Sharing Bear Hugs

Encouraging children to develop a love
of books helps their literacy now and makes a difference
to their whole future.

One of the main ways you can do this is by reading
aloud. It's never too early to start – even small babies enjoy
being read to – and it's important to carry on, even when
children can read for themselves.

Choose a time that suits you both and a place
that's comfortable.

Don't worry about being good at reading.
Your voice is one of the sounds your child loves best.
Encourage them to join in with rhymes or repeated phrases,
and to tell you the story in their own words.

Take time to look at the pictures together.
Pictures help tell the story that's written, but often
tell their own stories too.

It's a good sign if children comment and ask questions as
you read. It shows they're interested. Talk about the book.
Was it good? Were there any favourite moments?

Read aloud as often as you can – new stories
and old favourites!

For Jessica and Alice

First published 1990 by Walker Books Ltd
87 Vauxhall Walk, London SE11 5HJ

This edition produced 2002 for
The Book People Ltd, Hall Wood Avenue,
Haydock, St Helens WA11 9UL

2 4 6 8 10 9 7 5 3 1

This book has been typeset in Helvetica.

Printed in Hong Kong

British Library Cataloguing in Publication Data
A catalogue record for this book is available from the British Library.

ISBN 0-7445-6847-1

Bramble
AND THE
Big Storm

Benedict Blathwayt

TED SMART

Bramble was a very calm and
contented cow – most of the time.
But she hated loud noises …

like combine harvesters …

or bird scarers …

or jets.

They made her want to run away and hide.

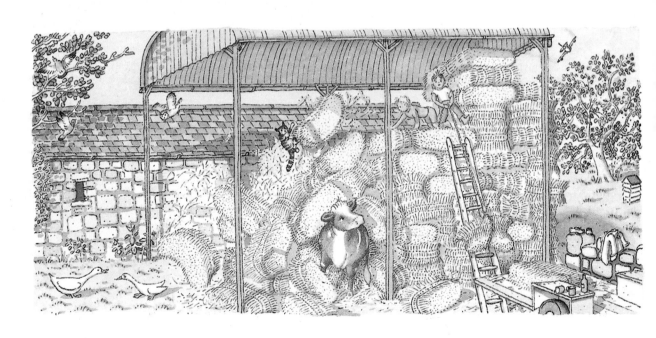

One day as she lay dozing in the hot sun,
some ducks flew low overhead, quacking loudly.

Bramble leaped up in fright. She jumped
straight over the wall ...

and landed in the pond. "Hello, Bramble!" shouted
the children. Mrs Warren wasn't very pleased.

Bramble was moved to the orchard
to calm down. But – what's that buzzing?
thought Bramble nervously.

She felt sure it was coming after her.
Where should she hide?

"Hello, Bramble!" cried Mrs Warren, very cross
indeed to find a cow in her kitchen. "What are we
going to do with you?" she said in despair.

That night there was a tremendous storm.
Farmer Warren led Bramble in from the field.
He knew all the noise would upset her.

"You can stay in there with your friends," he said.
"And *try* to be good."

The wind grew more and more fierce. Bramble
hated it moaning and whistling.

She tried to stay calm but it was
no use; she just had to escape. CRASH!
Bramble had a favourite hiding-place,
perfect for a wild night like this.

In the morning Farmer Warren found her.
Bramble expected a scolding.
"Hello, Bramble!" he said cheerfully.

"Hello, Bramble!" called Mrs Warren with a smile.
No one seemed cross about the broken door.

Then Bramble saw what the storm had done.

"The tree would have squashed you all flat if you hadn't run away," said Farmer Warren. Everyone was so pleased to see Bramble safe and sound, they forgot all the trouble she had caused.

Bear Hugs is a range of bright and lively picture books by some of today's very best authors and illustrators. Each book contains a page of friendly notes on reading and is perfect for parents and children to share.

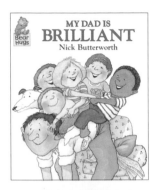

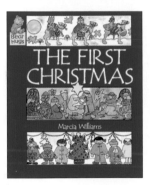

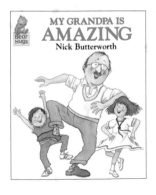

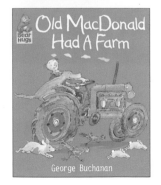

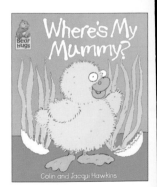

Cuddle up with a Bear Hug today!